PUSHKIN

Pushkin
Meets the Bundle

BY Harriet M. Ziefert   **ILLUSTRATED BY Donald Saaf**

AN ANNE SCHWARTZ BOOK

ATHENEUM BOOKS for YOUNG READERS

To William Ezra Ziefert
—H. M. Z.

For Julia
—D. S.

Atheneum Books for Young Readers
An imprint of Simon & Schuster Children's Publishing Division
1230 Avenue of the Americas
New York, New York 10020

Book design by Michael Nelson

The text of this book is set in Stempel Schneidler.
The illustrations are rendered in gouache.

First Edition
Printed in China for Harriet Ziefert, Inc.
10 9 8 7 6 5 4 3 2 1

Library of Congress Cataloging-in-Publication Data
Ziefert, Harriet.
Pushkin meets the bundle / Harriet M. Ziefert ; illustrated by Donald Saaf.—1st ed.
p. cm.
"An Anne Schwartz book."
Summary: Pushkin the dog, once the apple of his owners' eyes,
tries to cope with the arrival of a new baby to the house.
ISBN 0-689-81413-5
[1. Dogs—Fiction. 2. Babies—Fiction.] I. Saaf, Donald, ill. II. Title.
PZ7.Z487Pu   1998
[E]—dc21
96-37748

I am Pushkin.

I live with Kate and Michael on a quiet
street in a quiet neighborhood.

Here we are in the front yard,
just the three of us.

In the morning Kate and Michael go
to work. I stay home.
"Be a good boy," Michael always says.

And I usually am.

In the evening Kate and Michael
come home.

Kate takes me for a nice walk
while Michael cooks dinner.

I eat first.
"Slow down, Pushkin!" Kate says.

After dinner, Michael and I wrestle.

Or play ball.

Or practice tricks.

Then it's time for bed.
"Good night, Pushkin," says Kate.
"Sweet dreams."

"Sleep tight, big boy," says Michael.
"We love you."

I'm happy, till the day everything changes.
One evening Kate and Michael
do not come home.

There is no nice walk.

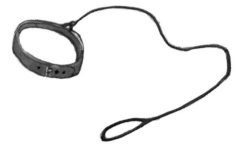

There is no delicious dinner.

I'm scared! Where *is* everybody?

Finally, they're back—Kate, Michael,
and a little bundle.

I try to say hello, but they are
too busy with the bundle.

Kate takes the bundle to our bedroom.
I watch her unwrap it.
It's a baby.

I am sent to sleep in the guest room.

Now every morning Michael lets me out.
"Make it quick, Pushkin," he says.

I think of running away.

After a while, Michael goes back to work.
I wish he would take the baby with him.
But he doesn't.

Kate stays home.
She pats the baby, but
she doesn't pat me.

She plays with the baby, but
she doesn't play with me.

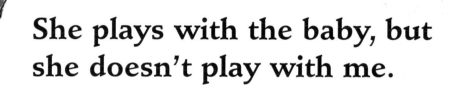

She kisses
the baby,
but she
doesn't
kiss me.

"Look at me!" I howl.
"Remember me? I'm Pushkin!"

"Sshhh!" says Kate. "You'll scare the baby!"

Well, *I* can be quiet, but this baby can't!
He has a big, BIG cry.

Michael and I can't practice our tricks.
Kate and I can't listen to music.

Just when *I'm* about to cry, I get a good idea.
"Watch me!" I say.
     And they do. All three of them.

I do my best tricks ever.

Kate and Michael clap and clap.
Then I hear a little laugh.
Are my ears playing tricks?

It's the baby!

I think I might just get
to like this baby after all.